Saint George
and the
Dragon

Retold by Louie Stowell

Illustrated by John Joven

Reading consultant: Alison Kelly
University of Roehampton

Contents

This is a famous painting of George in action. Turn to page 46 to find out more.

Chapter 1

The deadly dragon

A king was strolling on his battlements one day. As he admired his kingdom, he saw a dark shape in the distance.

It came
closer...

and closer...

Oh no!

4

and closer...

It was a dragon! Its eyes flashed like fire as it flew. It let out a mighty roar and...

...jets of yellow flame shot from its mouth and nose.

The king screamed. "HELP! Guards! To the roof, now!"

The dragon soared in a loop around the castle. It roared again and a river far below dried up with a sizzle.

The king's guards rushed onto the roof to see what the king was shouting about.

The dragon roared once
more and set five fields on fire.
The guards stared in horror.

"Stop that dragon!" ordered
the king. "It's going to burn us
all to cinders."

His guards hastily fired
their bows as the dragon
swooped through the sky.
Arrows flew
through the air.

Each arrow hit the dragon but then...

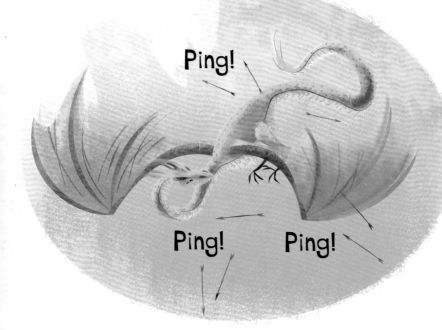

The arrows all bounced off the dragon's tough scales. The dragon laughed. "You can't hurt me! But feed me once a day and I'll leave you alone."

The king agreed. What else
could he do?

"Bring food to the cave by
the lake," said the dragon and,
with one last roar, it flew away.

Chapter 2

Feeding the beast

The next morning, the king's guards crept to the cave. They left two fat, juicy sheep for the dragon to eat.

When they came back the next day, the sheep were gone.

The dragon ate two sheep a day until there wasn't a sheep left in the kingdom.

"We'll have to feed it cows instead," sighed the king.

The next morning, guards brought the dragon two cows. As they were leaving, the dragon opened an eye and scowled.

I don't like cows!

"Bring me something else to eat," it said, "or I'll burn your kingdom to the ground."

So the guards ran to a nearby farm and fetched some plump young chickens.

"How about these?" said the leader of the guards.

Yuck!

"I hate chickens!" snarled the dragon. "Bring me something else."

The guards left again and came back with pigs and goats instead. Luckily, the dragon liked those.

Unluckily, it swallowed them down in a few gulps. "I'm still hungry," it grumbled.

"Bring me a princess," roared the dragon. "I want something sweet for a change."

"And don't pretend you don't have any princesses," it added, glaring at the guards. "I know the king has a daughter. I saw her as I flew over his castle."

"Bring her to me tomorrow at sunrise," the dragon went on, "or I'll burn the kingdom to the ground."

And it let out a burst of white-hot flame to show that it meant what it said.

The guards rushed back to tell the king the terrible news.

Chapter 3

Princess in peril

When the king heard the
dragon's threat, he went white.
"I won't allow it," he declared.
"Not my daughter!"

"But father, I have to go,"
said the princess. "Or he'll
burn us all!"

The king knew she was right.
With a heart as heavy as lead,
he ordered his grooms to get
the princess's horse ready.

Early the next morning, the
princess rode to the dragon's
cave. It was fast asleep. The
princess saw its sharp, pointed
teeth and shuddered with fear.

As the sun rose pink over
the hills, she heard the sound
of hooves. Was it her father
coming to say a last goodbye?

But it wasn't the king. It
was a handsome knight on
a beautiful white horse.

He carried a long lance in one hand. When he saw her, he gave a cheerful grin.

Hello! I'm George.

"I heard about the dragon," he said. "I'm here to help." The princess was overjoyed.

"Don't be afraid, Princess,"
George yelled. He swished his
lance. "I'll save you!"

"Thank you, George," the
princess whispered.

"But please," she added, "could you be as quiet as possible as you ride closer? Or you'll wake the..."

ROAAAAAAAR!

Too late! The dragon reared up on its scaly legs. It was awake and ready for a fight.

Chapter 4

George to the rescue

George whirled around to face the dragon. Flames shot out of its nose. They licked at George but he didn't move away.

Instead, he thrust his lance with a powerful blow. It should have skewered the dragon right through...

...but this dragon's skin was as hard as diamonds.

George's lance bounced off the dragon's belly, pushing George back. He fell from his horse to the ground, with a clattering thump.

The dragon roared, and spat another fiery cloud at George.

The princess looked on in terror. Was her rescuer going to need rescuing himself?

George started to stagger to his feet. He reached for his lance, ready to charge again.

It was no good. George's lance bounced off the dragon's scales and he fell to the ground once more.

"George, look!" the princess cried, all of a sudden. "There aren't any scales on its nose."

George peered closer. Sure enough, the dragon's nose was soft. It didn't have any scales there at all.

"Well spotted, Princess!" said George. But, as he prepared to attack, the dragon began to lash its head from side to side.

George looked around and had an idea. "Princess, pull off your belt, tie a loop at the end and pass it to me."

The princess was puzzled, but she did as he asked.

"Thank you, Princess!" said George.

He swung her belt around like a lasso and threw the loop over the dragon's head. Then he pulled it tight and threw the end to the princess.

"Hold on!" ordered George, and leaped onto his horse.

Before the dragon knew what was happening, George charged with his sharp lance.

With the princess holding
the dragon's head, George
speared its soft nose. Blood
spurted out.

The dragon howled in pain. It gave a great roar and tried to break free, but it was well and truly caught.

"Now dragon," said George, "I'll let you go if you promise me you'll leave this kingdom and never, ever eat a human."

The dragon nodded sulkily.

"But if I hear that you're breaking your promise..." said George, pointing to his lance.

The dragon took the hint and flew away as fast as its wings would carry it.

Chapter 5

A hero's reward

George and the princess rode back to the castle and told the king the whole story.

"You saved my darling daughter!" cried the king. "How can I ever repay you?"

He offered George a heap
of shining golden coins. "You
could buy your own castle."

"No thank you," said
George, shaking his head.
"Gold is too heavy to carry
when I'm on an adventure."

"Hmm," said the king, and he offered George a pair of fine horses. Their bridles were studded with gems and their coats gleamed like moonlight.

"Thank you, Sire," George said, "but I have a horse."

"How about half of my kingdom?" said the king, who was running out of ideas.

"No thank you," said George, politely. "All I really want is another adventure."

And with that, George rode off into the distance, looking for more dragons to defeat.

41

Stories of George

The George in this story may have been a soldier, born in Cappadocia (now in Turkey) in the third century.

Over the years, lots of different legends grew up about him.

Many of these were about a fight with a dragon. In some, the dragon's breath was poisonous. In others, George slayed the dragon on the spot.

The story was told aloud for many years before it was written down. It changed along the way, as it was told and retold.

Saint George

One of the earliest versions of George's story appeared in *The Golden Legend*, a collection of stories about Christian saints written in around 1260.

A saint is a person who lives a pure, good life. George was made a saint by the Christian church after he died.

George was adopted as the national saint of England in the 13th century. He is a saint of other countries, and cities too. This map shows some of them.

Map of Europe   Lithuania   Moscow

England

Barcelona
Portugal

Genoa

Malta and Gozo

Greece   Georgia

His feast day (a type of holy festival) is celebrated across the world, usually on April 23rd.

Saint George and the Dragon by Paolo Uccello (1397-1475)
National Gallery, London, England

George's story
has inspired
painters and
storytellers
for hundreds
of years.

This painting
is by an Italian
artist named
Paolo Uccello.
He created
it in around
1470.

You can see
the same scene
in this book on
pages 34-35.

Usborne Quicklinks

For links to websites where you can find out more about George and the dragon, and to see other paintings inspired by the tale, go to the Usborne Quicklinks Website at **www.usborne-quicklinks.com** and type in the keyword 'George'.

Please follow the internet safety guidelines on the Usborne Quicklinks Website. Usborne Publishing cannot be responsible for the content of any website other than its own. We recommend that children are supervised when using the internet.

Designed by Caroline Spatz
Series editor: Lesley Sims
Series designer: Russell Punter

First published in 2012 by Usborne Publishing Ltd., Usborne House, 83-85 Saffron Hill, London EC1N 8RT, England. www.usborne.com
Copyright © 2012 Usborne Publishing Ltd.
Pages 2 & 47 Uccello, Paolo (1397-1475): Saint George and the Dragon, about 1470. London, National Gallery. Oil on canvas, 55.6 x 74.2 cm. Bought with a special grant and other contributions, 1959. Acc.n.: 1617. © 2011. Copyright The National Gallery, London/Scala, Florence.